Dear Evie and Eddie,
Here is a little gift for Tallulah ♡.
I really hope you enjoy it and please let me know who will be your favourite fairy ♡
With much love, kindness + sprinkles of fairy dust -
XX Roberta XX

Written by Roberta Brown

Illustrated by Lorna Humphreys

First Edition 2022

Tallulah

ISBN: 978 1 3999 4330 7

Acknowledgement

I would like to thank Lorna Humphreys who skillfully brought Tallulah to life. Such a talented illustrator and without her there would be no finished book. I wrote Tallulah 18 years ago and finally after many life hurdles it is finally alive.

I am dedicating this book to my sons Sol, Sam and Ben. Thank you for all the lessons you still continue to teach me. Now young men in your twenties, independent, kind and motivated - you all make me proud to be your Mum.

To my wonderful friend Sue who introduced me to the world of dyslexia, supported me during some very hard times and of course helped me edit Tallulah. Thank you.

To my mum who always told me 'there was nothing I couldn't achieve' I am finally believing this.

Tallulah

Written by

ROBERTA BROWN

Illustrated by

LORNA HUMPHREYS

Once Upon a Fairy

Close your eyes and dream
Imagine what you'll see
Fairies in Tallulah's land
Dancing happily

Queen Tallulah's strict but fair
She sits upon her throne
Teaching the young fairies
How to fly alone

She's dressed in silk with silver beads
Her wings are made of lace
When Tallulah's feeling happy
A smile rests upon her face

Tallulah is the Queen
She's lived for many years
If fairies don't respect her rules
Her wrath will bring on tears

Every night around the world
A fairy takes a flight
It could be you or someone else
Who hides a tooth at night

You soon will learn a secret
Which you will have to keep
Never tell a soul
Not even in your sleep

Come let's meet Tallulah
And all her fairy girls
On white fluffy clouds
Dancing fairy twirls

The Fairies

First there's Libby-Lilly
A very clever thing
Silver boots and glasses
And an extra special wing

Daisy flower in her hair
A book held in her hand
Little Libby-Lilly
Is the smartest in the land

Tilly-Tulip so tiny and so small
The youngest fairy of them all
Dressed in pink with dainty shoes
So eagerly she waits for news

Tilly is the sweetest
She floats high in the sky
Very soon her time will come
When she will learn to fly

Ruby-Rose oh Ruby-Rose
Likes to scream and shout
Constantly complaining
Read on you'll soon find out

Pixie-Petal loves rainbows
And dreams for rain and sun
She flies high and longs for
A rainbow to bring some fun

The Fairy of the Night

When night arrives it's time to know
Who will be chosen to fly?
Tallulah gives her reasons
And tells the fairies why

"Good deeds are a must in Fairyland
You have to earn your flight
If I think you're worthy
Then I will grant the night"

Tallulah is looking for kindness
She wants the fairies to share
Be kind and giving she tells them
She wants them all to care

The fairies often scream and shout
It makes Tallulah sad
Jealousy in Tallulah land
Is often rather bad

"I've told you" Queen Tallulah says
"You fairies mustn't fight
For if you do the sparkly stars
Won't brighten up the night"

Castles made of teeth
Scatter across the sky
Tallulah's making a village
Where fairies learn to fly

The prize for a fairy that takes the tooth
And leaves the child to dream
Is the biggest bowl you've ever seen
Of fairy pink ice cream

Tallulah with her perfect face
Looks through her magic cloud
She sees a desperate boy
Talking very loud

Tallulah looks some more
She knows what she must do
The fairies close their eyes and sing
"We're on our way to you"

Libby-Lilly looked and saw
The boy behind the bathroom door
Pixie-Petal took a peek
Ruby-Rose began to shriek

All the fairies gathered round
Tallulah saw beyond
The little boy was struggling
Tallulah tapped her wand

The voice of the boy
Rose to the cloud
The fairies heard him
Yelling loud

The Boy

"My tooth is so wobbly
Why won't it budge?
It didn't even fall out
When I ate my brother's fudge"

"I'm only six but I can't wait
I'll have to do it quick
It has to happen here and now
Or I will be quite sick"

"My Mum keeps asking 'What's the rush?
It's just a little tooth'
But I've been waiting patiently
That really is the truth"

"Nighttime comes I count to three
My fingers do the rest"
Wibble wobble wibble
"I really try my best"

The boy shouts "Ouch I won't give up
I'll give a little tug"
Wibble wobble wibble
"I'm feeling rather smug"

"Hooray hooray I did it"
The tooth now in my hand
Time to meet Tallulah
Back in fairyland"

Time for Bed

Nighttime comes the stars are out
His tooth is shining bright
Wrapped in tissue beside his head
The boy turns out his light

Under his pillow he hides it
Awaiting a wonderful prize
Being rather sleepy
He has to close his eyes

Tick-tock tick-tock
He knows he'll have to wait
Hurry up Tallulah
It's getting really late

He falls asleep and starts to dream
Tallulah calls the flight
Tallulah Tallulah
Turn on the fairy light

SPACE
ROCKETS

Midnight

The night was dark the stars were bright
Tallulah sang her tune
And one-by-one the fairies came
And danced beneath the moon

Pixie-Petal Ruby-Rose flew quickly to their Queen
Libby-Lilly Tilly-Tulip were nowhere to be seen
"Hurry now" Tallulah sang "We have to travel far
Pixie-Petal tonight's your night come sit upon my star"

Ruby-Rose huffed and puffed
She gave a deep long sigh
"Don't be sad" said Libby-Lilly
"You'll get your chance to fly"

"My chance has gone" said Ruby-Rose
"Pixie-Petal stole my night
I won't give up that easily
I'll switch the fairy light"

"What do you mean?" said Libby-Lilly
"What fairy light and where?"
"Forget it Libby-Lilly
Don't pretend you care"

You see fairies in Tallulah's land
Had troubles of their own
The thing that fairies hate the most
Is being all alone

Pixie-Petal was so sweet
Tallulah loved her so
Rainbow-coloured wings and hat
Made Pixie steal the show

Big blue eyes skin so fair
Cheeks that could go pop
Nothing made Pixie-Petal
Ever want to stop

Pixie-Petal was so thrilled
She spun around to dance
"Oh thank you Queen Tallulah
For giving me this chance"

"I know that I'm too noisy
Livelier than the rest
But even so I promise
Tonight I'll do my best"

The man in the moon winked with his eye
"Pixie my darling it's time to fly"
Off with a flutter she flew out of sight
Like a torpedo into the night

The Bedroom

The sleeping boy lay dreaming
Pixie-Petal flew inside
She flapped her wings together
And found a place to hide

For fairies have to hide at first
And take a look around
They must be very careful
Not to make a sound

The man in the moon winked with his eye
"Pixie my darling it's time to fly"
Off with a flutter she flew out of sight
Like a torpedo into the night

The Bedroom

The sleeping boy lay dreaming
Pixie-Petal flew inside
She flapped her wings together
And found a place to hide

For fairies have to hide at first
And take a look around
They must be very careful
Not to make a sound

Pixie-Petal felt sleepy
She lay upon the floor
When suddenly she noticed
Something at the door

Very still she kept
She didn't move at all
When she saw the shadow
It was really rather small

Pixie-Petal looked and saw
The shadow moving at the door
She looked again and rubbed her eyes
This really was a bad surprise

The Fairy Fight

Ruby-Rose had followed her
On Pixie's special night
"Why are you here?" she whispered
Determined not to fight

Ruby-Rose just stood and laughed
And with her eyes she stared
"Queen Tallulah sent me here
To try and make you scared"

"I'm not afraid of you
You're just a sad red fairy
There is nothing you could do
To make me think you're scary"

Ruby-Rose was getting cross
Her face was red as fire
"I do hope Pixie-Petal
You're not calling me a liar"

"For though Tallulah loves you most
The others hate you so
Libby-Lilly forced me here
She wanted you to know"

"Oh no oh no this can't be true
We know how you do lie"
All the fairies in the land
Know that Ruby's sly

"Believe what you wish" said Ruby-Rose
Tonight I'll take this tooth
When we return to Tallulah Land
You'll soon find out the truth"

Pixie-Petal was frightened
Ruby-Rose was really strong
But Pixie-Petal was tougher
And Ruby was in the wrong

As Ruby-Rose flew over
To the sleeping child's bed
Pixie-Petal made a dash
And grabbed at Ruby's head

"You're hurting me" screamed Ruby-Rose
"You're tearing at my wings"
"Then learn tonight Miss Ruby-Rose
You can't go stealing things"

Suddenly a sprinkle of salt
Came tumbling to the floor
Queen Tallulah was staring a stare
Like no one had seen before

Tallulah's face was raging
Her wand was in her hand
Nothing made Tallulah
Leave the fairy land

"What are you doing?" she asked
Pixie started to cry and she knew
"Ruby-Rose had followed me
I didn't know what to do"

The Fairy Punishment

Tallulah closed her eyes
And sang her famous song

"Your power must be returned to me
Now come and take my hand
No more flying Ruby-Rose
You have betrayed the land"

Ruby-Rose tried to fly away
Tallulah threw her spell
Ruby-Rose came crashing down
Above her black dust fell

Queen Tallulah looked to see
Her eyes now warm and bright
"I'm sorry for the trouble
That you have had tonight"

Pixie-Petal was quivering
Her wings a little frail
Her puffed up rosy cheeks
Had turned a little pale

The Tooth

Pixie-Petal saw the clock
It was almost nearly two
She had to get the tooth
She knew just what to do

Pixie-Petal flew up high
She landed on the bed
Oh so gently without a sound
She lifted the boy's head

Pixie-Petal looked at him
She saw his dreamy eyes
One two three she took the tooth
And left him his surprise

"I've done it I've done it
It's the best tooth I've seen
I must hurry back
To my Fairy Queen"

Twilight-time in the land
Most fairies drift and dream
But all that Pixie-Petal wants
Is fairy pink ice cream

A smile broke out on Pixie's face
She knows her flight is done
The man in the moon winks again
It's time for the morning sun

The Fairy Party

There on the star is Tallulah
So gracious as she waits
By her side Pixie sees
Fairy china plates

Libby-Lilly squeals
She wakes the others too
But Ruby-Rose still can't move
There's nothing she can do

Dawn begins the fairies stretch
They see the morning light
This tooth now in Tallulah's hand
Is a magic type of white

"I'm sorry I'm sorry
I truly am indeed"
Ruby-Rose was crying
She was desperate to be freed

Tallulah held her wand
She blinked her crystal eyes
"Ruby-Rose please promise now
There must be no more lies"

"I promise Queen Tallulah
I've learnt a lot tonight
No one likes a fairy
That always wants to fight"

The fairy pink ice cream
Was eaten with delight
The man in the moon winked again
For morning was his night

The magic cloud reappeared
The boy rose from his sleep
He moved his patchwork pillow
To have a little peep

"WOW" said the boy "a real fairy gift
I can't believe my eyes
A teeny weeny telescope
For me to see the skies"

At last the boy was happy
He thought it was a dream
The fairies danced and giggled
Full of pink ice cream

"Who will be next Tallulah?"
But Tallulah will not say
"The kindest fairy I will choose
But on another day"

The End

About the Author

Roberta Brown is a mindfulness life coach also known as 'The Mindful Mum Of London'. She has been writing poems since she was ten years old. When Roberta's youngest was diagnosed with dyslexia she decided to learn all she could to assist him in his school life.

For one year Roberta travelled 3 hours every Friday to attend a course which would give her the skill set needed to guide her son. He is now 21 and in his last year at a top London University after having obtained top grades in both his GCSE's and A Levels.

Roberta believes that every child deserves to be given the opportunity to be the best they can be and this book has been written with a specific font ideal for children who find reading difficult. '

When another of Roberta's sons lost his tooth he was too scared to meet the tooth fairy so he put his tooth under his pillow and slept in another bedroom. Roberta found this hilarious and wrote a letter from the fairy saying how sad she was that he wasn't there in his bed and therefore she couldn't leave his gift. The following night, back in his own bedroom and tooth under his pillow the fairy came. This was the moment Tallulah was born. This was 2004, her son was 6 years old. Tallulah has waited patiently for 18 years and finally here she is with her 4 magnificent fairies.

Roberta is well known for writing poems and was nominated to write a poem a day for 21 days. Each poem is unique and moving. Soon to be out on Amazon so keep your eyes open for "My Life In Words "

Her sons consider her to be an award winning mother and poet, a great cook, exceptionally kind with a wonderful sense of humour and vivid imagination.
She has an incredible gift when it comes to writing poems that rhyme, are imaginative and teach young children about compassion, empathy and diversity.

Roberta lives in London with her Golden Doodles who she loves and is forever grateful for the people in her life who have supported her journey.